WARNING

This book contains sexually explicit scenes and adult language. It may be considered offensive to some readers. This book is for sale to adults ONLY.

* * * * * * * * * * * * * * * * * *

Please store your files wisely where they cannot be accessed by underage readers.

Other Books by Carla Coxwell:

<u>Torrid Exposure New Adult Romance Series</u>

April is finished with school and ready to build a career. Coming from a well-to-do family, she has decided to reboot her life completely. With family scars too deep to mend, April craves a fresh start. But the past is harder to shake than April ever would have imagined. At the center of it all is Bennett, an old family friend who is the heir to a billionaire media mogul company. Bennett and April haven't been able to stand each other since they were kids. But as the world shifts, the two of them discover the past might be the key to their future.

<u>Devil's Advocate BBW MC New Adult Romance Series</u>

When Kristie comes home from college, the last thing she is expecting is her world to be turned upside down by the appearance of her step-brother, Gray. Gray is rash, impulsive and breaks the law. Kristie's mom asks if she can try to befriend Gray, in hopes to get him on the straight and narrow. The plan backfires, however, as Kristie finds herself falling for Gray. Is it possible he feels the same way? The connection between them threatens to tear down everything Kristie has ever held dear.

<u>Fifty Recipes For Disaster New Adult Romance Series</u>

Trying to win a competition for best chef is cut-throat business. Kiara Sands has just won the opportunity of a lifetime. When she arrives at Fission, she has no idea just how much her life is going to change. She's immediately introduced to Jenny Foster and Robbs Martin, her competitors in the cut throat competition. The only thing Kiara finds more distracting than Robbs' hateful attitude is the handsome executive chef, Paul Weston. It doesn't help matters that Paul is quite taken by Kiara, and showers her with more attention than he gives her competitors.

<u>Star Bright New Adult Romance Series</u>

Torn between her feelings for her agent, Jon, and Rich, a charming bad boy who has ties in the movie industry, Jenny finds herself working through her own past to try to get a grip on her present. As she struggles to learn the lesson that in Hollywood not everyone is what they appear to be, Jenny tries to become a person that she can be proud of. Will she be able to find love and success in Hollywood? Or will she be dragged down by her past forever?

Get the latest update on new releases from the author at:

https://www.carlacoxwell.com/newsletter

This book is Part One of the "Obsessed Bounty Hunter Romance Series"

1 - Secrets Revealed

Jacqui Schneider couldn't help it. Every time the memories of her family's brutal murder haunted her, she had to escape. The only thing that could replace her sorrow was sex... and lots of it. And so Jacqui developed a pattern of self-destruction by sleeping with random men that she picked up at a local hotel bar. One day, Uncle Max, an old family friend, appeared. He revealed a secret about her father that would change her life forever.

2 - Heart Surrendered

Jaqui thought the training was tough. But keeping her mind concentrated on her task was even tougher after meeting her new trainer. Adam had a rugged handsome face and ripped abs. She hated that Adam was so demanding. Jacqui's boxing technique was never up to his standards. How can she hate someone so much and yet feel such strong attraction? Was he flirting with her while trying to show her the correct stance? If so, the game of seduction was on.

3 - Rapid Pulse Bounty

With her new skills fully developed, Jacqui was a confident bounty hunter with a few successful captures under her belt. Things were looking up for her. The only thing missing in her life right now was Adam. She hadn't seen him since before her first successful mission. He had left before she could show off her triumph. Jacqui admitted to herself that she was in love with a man who belonged to someone else.

Obsessed Bounty Hunter Romance Series

Secrets Revealed

Book One

By Carla Coxwell

Table of Contents

Chapter One

JACQUI SCHNEIDER awoke with a sudden start, the unfamiliarity of her surroundings sending waves of panic sweeping all through her body. Her head whipped frantically from side to side as her eyes swept across the shadowy interior.

She could see the white sheer curtain drawn across the glass window. The sky outside the window had a purplish hue, indicating the first blush of dawn. A console table just below the window held a tray with a thermos bottle and a cup and saucer set neatly stacked beside it. A beige telephone and a digital clock with the time displayed as 4:27 a.m. rested on the other side of the console table. She recognized her clothes as they lay strewn on the floor. Her high-heeled shoes and purse lay in a pile near the door.

She was in a hotel room. As awareness took over, Jacqui was glad her sudden movement did not disturb the sleeping form beside her. She glanced at the figure snoring softly and saw his hand reach out for her. He stirred, breathing deeply, and then resumed his sleep. Jacqui hoped he would not notice the empty space beside him as she tiptoed silently out of bed and gathered her clothes from the floor.

Jacqui wanted to leave the hotel before the man woke up. Things were less complicated that way. She couldn't even remember his name. Was it John… or Jack… or Jim…?

Jacqui didn't really care. It was strictly sexual. She had no intention of ever seeing him again. He was just a random guy she had picked up in the hotel bar last night. The guys were always the same. Non-threatening, married, from out of town, and only out to have a good time. A few made a play of removing their wedding rings. But Jacqui could always spot the telltale lighter skin tone where the ring used to be.

This suited Jacqui just fine. It wasn't a good idea to hook up with someone local. She always made sure the guy was at the hotel for a convention, or just an overnight stay. She usually spotted them because of the name tag pinned over their breast pocket. She'd sit in the bar with her drink, until someone struck up a conversation or offered her a drink.

Jacqui was very hard not to notice. She was tall and lithe and had full breasts, milky white skin, and a nice round ass. She had sparkling green eyes, high cheekbones and luscious lips, topped by chestnut brown hair that fell softly to her shoulders; she attracted instant attention. And this guy…Jim…Jacqui suddenly remembered, was no different. He made a beeline for her as soon as he spotted her at the bar.

"Hi, my name's Jim… I hope you don't mind the intrusion…" Jacqui remembered him saying. "But it looks like your glass needs a refill." Jacqui gave him a

smile. It was the standard pickup line. He didn't know
she already pegged him through the glass mirrors lining
the liquor cabinet of the bar. He was going to be "it" for
tonight.

"Are you staying in this hotel?" Jim asked,
signaling the bartender for another shot of brandy for
her. "No…" Jacqui answered. "Are you waiting for
someone…?" Jim asked. Jacqui could read the
expectant look in his eyes, and this was usually her cue.
If she didn't like what she saw or if she had second
thoughts about her safety, she'd say… "Yes, I'm just
waiting for my boyfriend to pick me up…" Or offer
some other lame excuse.

But she had liked what she saw. Jim was tall, good-
looking and neatly dressed. And he had a ring on his
finger. "No…" Jacqui answered and gave him a flirty
smile. "My name is Nina…" she added. Yes, she would
be a horny Nina tonight, or Glenna, or Linda. It didn't
really matter. She just wanted to get laid. And tonight,
Jim was it.

Jacqui could predict how the next hour would play
out. Jim will tell her his life story as he kept filling up
her glass hoping to get her drunk enough so she would
be pliant when he made his move. The thought almost
made Jacqui laugh. The poor guy didn't know that was
exactly her plan.

"You've hardly told me anything about yourself,
Nina…" Jim complained playfully, as his hand dropped
down to her knee. "There's really nothing to tell…I'm
just a girl hoping to get lucky tonight…" Jacqui

whispered seductively in his ear. His hand moved a little further up her skirt as Jacqui opened her legs a little wider to allow him to feel her crotch through her sheer stockings. Jim's eyes opened wide in surprise as he felt the heat emanating through the silk.

"Why don't we finish this conversation upstairs in my room?" Jim asked. Jacqui nodded her head in reply as her bosom heaved in anticipation. This was the reason she was here tonight. This guy, Jim, would make her forget even for just a few hours, those thoughts and images that constantly lurked in her psyche, tormenting her. When they came uninvited, Jacqui knew what would make her forget. Sex.

Jacqui sashayed her way out of the bar ahead of him. She wanted him to see her firm ass, tapered waist, and long slim legs. It was hard to ignore the looks from other men that followed her and this aroused her even more. She made her way out and straight into the banks of elevators. Jim could hardly contain his excitement. His erection was bulging through his pants.

As soon as the bedroom door closed behind them, Jacqui dropped down on her knees and unzipped his pants. She grabbed hold of his cock. She spit down on it as her hands feverishly stroked it. Jim was hardly out of his pants before Jacqui had him inside her mouth. Jim threw back his head in arousal. He was stunned at the ferocity with which Jacqui moved her head back and forth, her saliva leaving his shaft red and glistening. Jacqui toyed with the head of his cock and tasted the sweet dew that signaled that he would cum prematurely if she didn't slow down.

And Jim didn't want to cum just yet. He had plans of sucking and tasting every inch of her. He would fuck her hard, until the tension building inside his body became unbearable, and then he would blow his load in her mouth. He pulled her up and began to unhook her bra. Jacqui's face was wild with anticipation as she shimmied out of her clothes and stockings. A slight sweat broke out in her armpits. Her boobs swelled as Jim groped one breast with his hand and twirled his thumb and forefinger around the sensitive nipple. Using his mouth, he sucked on the other nipple. Jacqui arched her back in pleasure as waves of ice and fire shot straight through to her groin.

Jim continued sucking her breast and nibbling her nipple with his teeth. His other hand traveled down her flat stomach. He stopped just below her mound, feeling the coarse pubes that covered her vagina. Using his fingers to separate the lips, he caressed her clit and discovered just how wet and aroused she was. Jim stroked her clit repeatedly. He slid in another finger, adding pressure with every stroke. He could feel the inner muscles of her vagina tightening each time his hand brushed against her swollen clitoris. Jacqui closed her eyes and moaned her pleasure. Getting fingered felt really good.

But Jacqui knew she wanted more than his fingers. Pulling him along, she lay back against the bed and opened her thighs. Her pussy was slick with her own juice. "Do you like what you see?" she whispered up at him as Jim nodded. "Eat me. Show me what your tongue can do…" she whispered huskily as she caressed herself to arouse him. Jacqui grabbed her knees and spread her legs even wider for him, leaning her head back against the pillow. Her invitation was obvious, insistent.

Jim scrambled up the bed, his erect penis bouncing with the movement. Then he knelt down between her legs, enthralled with the red-hot pussy before him. He lowered his head as his hands separated the lips of her vagina, exposing the engorged clit. He flicked his tongue against it as Jacqui's body heaved with pleasure. He flicked repeatedly; mesmerized by the guttural sounds emanating from Jacqui's mouth each time his rough tongue made contact with the sensitive skin.

She began to moan as he went faster and faster until finally she couldn't take it anymore. She wanted to feel his cock inside her. Jim positioned himself on top of her. He used his elbows to steady himself as his cock searched for her vagina's opening. Jacqui savored the feeling of the velvety skin of his cock rubbing against the slick wetness of her clit. Jim rammed himself inside her. And then he drew back until the head of his cock was barely past the opening of her vaginal wall. Then he rammed into her once again, filling her completely.

Jacqui flattened her heels against the hard muscle of Jim's buttocks, urging him to go faster and faster. She needed him to fuck her hard. It was what drove the demons away. Every thrust made her moan louder and louder. Her pussy was on fire. Tension swept all over her body and gathered within her groin. Unexpectedly, Jim flipped her over. Jacqui buried her face into the pillow. With her ass in the air, he entered her from behind. His hands reached out and groped her nipples.

The sensation of his fingers pinching and pulling her nipple while ramming her pussy was too much to bear. She knew she couldn't hold on much longer. She hoped that Jim was nearly there.

"I'm coming…" Jim grunted in her ear. The words were like fuel that ignited the raging fire from within. She gave in to a powerful orgasm that shook her body as she felt Jim shudder repeatedly behind her. After a couple of seconds, Jim lowered her gently on the bed as he withdrew from her and spooned her from behind. Jacqui got what she had come for. She was exhausted. She closed her eyes as languid exhaustion filled her completely. Sleep came within seconds. A dreamless sleep that held at bay all the horrors that she wanted to forget.

Chapter Two

Jacqui slid the key into the lock of her single storey house. The whole neighborhood was silent. She was glad no one was around to see her. She didn't need that kind of talk, especially since….

She glanced at the houses lining the street where she lived. Tall sycamore trees lined the sidewalk like silent sentinels. A child's red bike leaned haphazardly by the fence railing in one of the houses. A neighbor had left his garden sprinkler on and the water spray hitting the sunlight created a rainbow as it arced across the yard. Three houses down from hers, a teenaged boy riding his bike threw a newspaper that landed on the grass near the porch. A dog could be heard barking in the distance. It was a neighborhood that resembled myriad others all across America.

Jacqui sighed deeply. She was envious of her neighbors. Every night she imagined what it was like to be inside those homes. The warmth of sleeping bodies as they lay in bed, tucked warmly, cozy within the loving embrace of loved ones. Safe and secure.

Except for Jacqui. She hated coming home. And her front yard showed it. Tall weeds and grass covered the yard, badly in need of a trim. Her porch was littered with unread newspapers dating back to three months ago. She had paid the newspaper boy weeks ago and told him to stop coming. But she had never bothered to put away the dailies that now littered her porch. She was afraid to open them. She knew the headlines would just bring her back to those terrifying days.

Of course, she could hire someone to clean up for her. Guilty feelings assailed her because it didn't use to be this way. She felt embarrassed. But her neighbors seemed to understand. At least no one had complained yet. They were giving her time, she thought. The interior of the house wasn't so bad except for the accumulation of dust everywhere. Curtains permanently drawn against the windows allowed for very little sunlight as they hung listlessly against the glass panes. But for Jacqui it was a blessing. She didn't need to see the living room where it had all happened.

She tried calling Mrs. Evans once on the off-chance that she would agree to clean up for her. But instinctively, she knew the cleaning lady would say no. Jacqui couldn't really blame her. So she left things the way they were three months ago. The Crime Scene Clean-up Crew did a good job of removing the bloodstains. Jacqui was grateful for that. She avoided entering the dark living room or using the kitchen. But dust had a way of seeping through cracks in the floor and had accumulated everywhere. Jacqui didn't have the will to do anything about it.

Her footsteps echoed across the floor of the empty house as she walked toward her bedroom at the end of the hallway. She pushed open the bedroom door not even bothering to switch on the lights. What for? She knew her way around. Her room was her solace. The familiarity was comforting.

Right now, all she wanted was to take her clothes off and jump into the shower. Thank God she had her own bathroom. One of the perks her parents had gifted her when she decided to stay instead of getting her own place. She would report for work late today, she decided.

Her boss understood her situation and allowed her to come in anytime she wanted to. Heck, he even insisted she take a vacation and reassured her she would still have a job when she got back. Jacqui was grateful but adamant. She needed to fill the hours of her day. That… and she needed the money to survive.

Because of the darkness that surrounded her, Jacqui failed to see the figure watching her silently from the wingback chair pushed carelessly against the wall.

"Hello Jacqui…" the voice greeted her. Jacqui wheeled around in fright, her heart pounding wildly. The figure stood slowly and made its way to the light switch. "Uncle Max…? What…where…oh my God you scared me to death…" Jacqui stammered. She wanted to run to him and hug him. He was a familiar figure. A comforting presence. Someone she had known since she was a child. But suddenly, anger replaced the joy she felt in seeing Uncle Max again.

"What are you doing here?" she asked icily. "I came to see how you were doing," Uncle Max replied with calmness, so typical of the way Jacqui remembered him. "You came to see how I…?" Jacqui repeated as her anger turned to fury. "You didn't even come to their funeral. You were my dad's best friend. How could you do that? I called so many times but your phone was disconnected," Jacqui wailed. Tears of anger and frustration welled up in her eyes. "I couldn't, Jacqui…I couldn't afford for the Police and the FBI to make the connection," Uncle Max explained.

"Connection…? What are you talking about?" Jacqui demanded in an accusing voice. Uncle Max drew a deep breath and replied, "Jac, there are a lot of things you don't know. But believe me when I say that staying away… not saying goodbye for the last time…that was the hardest thing I ever did." Jacqui saw Uncle Max struggling to keep his emotions in check. Suddenly all the pent-up tears came rushing out. The intensity caught Jacqui by surprise and knocked the air out of her. Jacqui swayed as Uncle Max reached out to catch her. He held her tenderly as her silent tears gave way to heavy sobs which still did not manage to ease the pain that racked her heart. Incoherent words spewed from her lips as she relived the incident.

"It was frightening… I was in my room when I heard dad pleading to spare my mom… He was using his body to shield her. Mom was crying hysterically… struggling to get in front of my dad as if to shield him," Jacqui's voice cracked as she remembered. Then she continued, "The man had the gun pointed at his head… the gunshot was so silent. I didn't even realize he had fired. At first I thought it was my dad that got hit. But then I saw my mom topple over as dad screamed." A fresh wave of sobs made her voice incoherent. But Jacqui couldn't stop.

"Dad cradled my mom as she lay on the floor with a surprised look on her face. Then she reached out and touched dad's face. Dad just kept saying no…no…no…The killer did it on purpose, Uncle Max. He wanted my dad to see him murder my mom. And then…and then… Danny appeared from the kitchen. He still held a spoon in his hand. He was eating cereal. Uncle Max, I didn't even know my brother was home. I thought he was still in school. But he must have gotten sick and mom made him stay home. Then the man wheeled around and shot him too. He was just a kid…he was just a little boy."

The old man's shirt was drenched with her tears as the memory sent shockwaves of pain, remembering the bloody slaughter. Then Jacqui continued on, "My dad screamed with rage. Then he tried to grab the gun away. The man shot him in the head. He didn't even see me crouching behind the door. I wanted to scream for help, but I was frozen with terror. I couldn't move. Everything happened so fast. It felt like hours before I realized the man was gone. I crawled all the way to see them. There was blood everywhere. I didn't know I was screaming until the neighbors came."

Jacqui finally allowed months of pent up feeling to come out as she bawled and screeched her sorrow over the tragic murder of her family. Uncle Max held her gently, tenderly, allowing her tears to lighten the load she had carried all these months. After what seemed like an eternity, Jacqui's heaves eventually settled into quiet sobs, and then to silent sniffles, until she just lay exhausted in his arms.

"It's alright, baby girl, everything will be alright…" Uncle Max consoled her. Jacqui looked up and smiled into his face and said, "I'm glad you're here now." Uncle Max held her at arm's length and said, "We need to talk, Jac. Can we do that? There are things you need to know. Go take a shower. Change your clothes and come with me. There's an all-night café near the park where we can chat."

Jacqui nodded her head in agreement. She entered the bathroom, took a quick shower, and came out with a towel wrapped around her body. She rummaged through her closet for some clean clothes. "Aren't you going to give me some privacy while I change?" she asked. Uncle Max was relieved to hear the hint of amusement in her voice.

"I've changed your diapers since you were a baby. You've got nothing that I haven't seen," Uncle Max replied seriously. Jacqui smiled, took a pair of jeans and a light cashmere sweater and reentered the bathroom. In a couple of minutes she was out again, with her hair tied back into a ponytail. She was eager to hear what Uncle Max had to say. Maybe he had some ideas that could help the FBI and the Police. They had drawn a blank and the case had been shelved until a new lead could be found.

Uncle Max led the way out of her bedroom. Instead of going straight for the door, he walked into the living room and stood near the spot where her mom and dad and Danny died. He stood still except when he wiped away the tears from his eyes. And then he walked towards Jacqui and ushered her out the door. They strolled down two blocks and turned a corner where he approached a car that was parked by the sidewalk. Jacqui understood that he didn't want the neighbors to see him. Suddenly she realized there was so much she did not know about Uncle Max. Dad said they were together in the military until both were discharged. But even her dad didn't talk much about the past.

Uncle Max was a familiar figure that had come to visit through the years. A doting man they learned to call Uncle. He would stay for a couple of days here and there, and during those times, Jacqui remembered how happy his dad seemed to have him around. They would often talk in his study for hours. Her mom showered him with affection and treated him sweetly. Jacqui had always assumed he was a distant relative.

Still, Jacqui couldn't remember any stories about where he lived or if Uncle Max had family somewhere. It dawned on Jacqui that Uncle Max was the closest person to a family that she had. The thought left her feeling sad, but somehow at ease. At least for now he was here.

Chapter Three

Jacqui stared incredulously at the old man seated in front of her. Two empty mugs of coffee and a plate of sandwiches were the only witnesses to everything Uncle Max had said. He spoke in a low voice, eyes alert and constantly looking around. He would stop whenever someone came within earshot.

Jacqui felt her head would explode. She was stunned. She didn't know what to say. "I understand it's a bit much to take in all at once…" the old man said, seeing the bewilderment on her face. "A bit much? How about me realizing I didn't really know my dad after all these years. He was just…dad," Jacqui replied still in denial.

And then she continued in amazement, "My dad was a bounty hunter?" "Yup, one of the best. I recruited him and trained him," Uncle Max replied. The old man continued, "During the times he was away from you guys, he was out there tracking someone." Jacqui remembered the long absences from home. But mom always said dad had a job as a consulting engineer building bridges or making roads somewhere. Jacqui learned to accept it. Whenever he came home he was always exhausted and seemed to have lost weight. Jacqui concluded it was because he had worked very hard during his travels. But he always had presents for her and Danny. A token from one of the many places where he worked, he said.

And whenever he was around, he brought them everywhere - the mall, the dentist, to the doctor's office. He drove them to school every single day. He even cooked breakfast for them. He often joked he was giving mom a rest from all these chores because he was away a lot. And mom seemed like a changed woman whenever dad came home. She would smile more often unlike when he was away. She was always tense and irritable. Her mom was totally devoted to her dad.

Growing up, Jacqui had looked forward to his return every time he went away. Dad was cool and easygoing. He allowed them liberties while mom would just shake her head in disapproval. Now, she suddenly realized he was making up for his absences, grateful perhaps, that he had made it home safe and in one piece.

"Did mom know about his other job…his real job?" Jacqui asked. "Yes, your mom knew about it," Uncle Max replied. Jacqui whistled through her teeth. So it wasn't a secret. Her mom must have supported her dad all the way. Jacqui stared at her Uncle Max once again. She wouldn't have such a hard time accepting him as the bounty hunter, but not her dad. Uncle Max was tall and burly. Even at his age, almost 70 years old, Jacqui believed he could beat the shit out of any younger guy.

But remembering her dad, Jacqui found it hard to think so. Dad was never violent. He was shorter than Uncle Max, and wasn't the athletic type. Jacqui never saw him exercise or lift weights or do stuff that required much strength. "Shouldn't a bounty hunter be some kind of macho man, with bulging muscles… someone who can kick ass?" Jacqui inquired, still unable to go from the picture of the dad she knew to the man her Uncle Max spoke about.

"Jac, being a bounty hunter doesn't have anything to do with muscles or being the strongest man alive," Uncle Max informed her. "Your dad was one of the best because he had a sharp mind that he camouflaged by being ordinary. He could blend well in a crowd and not look suspicious. That was his strength. You'd be surprised how many fugitives we managed to capture because they thought he was just another guy they could push around. He wasn't intimidating to anyone," Uncle Max explained.

"But how did he protect himself when things went bad? I assume he must have had some sticky situations," Jacqui asked curiously. The old man gave this some thought before he replied. "Your dad was a dead shot with a firearm. He was a sharpshooter. He could take down anyone from fifty meters away. And besides, he said he was the fastest thing on foot when he needed to be."

Jacqui laughed at that. She did remember her dad running after a pickpocket who had snatched her mom's purse near the mall. He overtook the younger guy and tackled him to the ground. This also explained his one passion. He loved guns. He had a collection, but he always kept them under lock and key because of

Danny. But it was also through a gun that he had lost his life, and her mom's and Danny's too.

Uncle Max saw the sudden change in her expression and knew she was remembering that fatal day once again. He reached out his hand and clasped hers from across the table. "Jac, your dad left you some money. I want you to know that. You never need to work again or worry about your future as long as you decide to live simply." Jacqui looked up in surprise. She hadn't seen that coming.

"Your dad never touched a single cent of what he earned as a bounty hunter. And he earned a lot. He placed it all in a trust fund for you and Danny. He called it his 'what if something happens to me' money. But with Danny gone, it's all yours now. I hope you don't mind that I invested it in some bonds. Your dad agreed it was the best thing," Uncle Max said.

"How much money did he leave for me and Danny?" Jacqui was curious to know. "Here's the information on the accounts. The money is yours anytime you want," Uncle Max said, handing her a memory stick and a number scribbled on a piece of paper. Jacqui almost choked on the amount. She kept silent, her mind reeling over everything she just learned.

She looked all around her. The café was slowly filling up with early morning patrons ordering coffee on their way to work. Everything looked so ordinary. And yet it wasn't. She was now all alone in the world without a family to share her failures, her triumphs, or her plans for the future. She also happened to be rich because of the money dad had left her.

This made her think about her future plans. What was there for her to do? She was 24 years old and until three months ago, she was still living at home with her mom and dad. But that was because her mom had needed help to look after Danny whenever dad was away. But now they were all gone.

"Hmm….Bounty Hunter…" she murmured softly to herself. It sounded like something straight from a B movie. And she had lived with one for 24 years without knowing it. Suddenly she remembered something very important. "Uncle Max, was my family murdered because of this…this bounty hunter stuff?" Jacqui asked.

Uncle Max drew a sigh before he replied, "I believe so. Your dad was on the trail of a notorious arms dealer. He was posing as a supplier. He managed to set a meeting with the target. But the guy never showed. We concluded that your dad's cover was blown… perhaps the target acquired fresh information about who your dad really was."

"These guys are vicious, Jac. Vengeance is a common occurrence. It's a way of sending the message, 'you don't mess with us.' Your dad knew that. He lived knowing each job could be his last," the old man said. "Who's the guy, Uncle Max?" Jacqui asked curiously. She had an instinct that the old man knew something. Uncle Max sighed deeply. A troubled look marked his face.

He looked Jacqui in the eye and replied, "Jac, in my line of business there is information that is too sensitive to disclose. I can't tell you that. I have no proof and I answer to a higher authority. All we do is supply the name and whereabouts of the person we track. We get paid big money for that information. When one of us gets killed, everything connecting us to that person is erased. That's why you couldn't get in touch with me after your family was murdered."

Jacqui could hardly believe Uncle Max wasn't going to help her catch her family's killer. Yet a quiet acceptance started to dawn on her. Her dad had done this for a living. She had to respect that. He had known the risks he was taking and he prepared to face them. Her dad loved them so much, and had wanted to guarantee a good future for her and Danny. She was sure of that.

Uncle Max stood up. Jacqui knew this conversation was over and followed him out the door of the café. The old man thought it was best to go while he still had the will to keep silent. It would not do any good to let on more than Jacqui needed to know. Both were silent on the drive back home.

"You're leaving again," Jacqui said as Uncle Max reached the driveway to her house. She hoped he could stay longer, although she noticed there was no luggage to indicate a longer visit. "Yes, baby girl…" Uncle Max replied as he searched for something in the backseat of the car.

His hand drew out a cell phone, which he handed to
Jacqui. Jacqui looked at it curiously. "Call me if you
need anything. Use this… but only to call me. No one
should know about this phone. Hide it. Is that
understood?" Uncle Max asked. Jacqui nodded her
head, acknowledging that she understood. She tucked
the phone into the pocket of her pants and stepped out
of the car.

"I love you, Uncle Max," Jacqui said through the
window. "Love you too, baby girl," Uncle Max replied
before driving away, glancing at the receding figure of
Jacqui through the rearview mirror. Jacqui stepped into
the threshold of the house, caressing the phone that
bulged through the pocket of her pants. She walked into
the living room and drew the curtains aside to let the
sunshine in.

As light flooded into the room, Jacqui felt less
lonely for the first time in a long time. Things will
change, she thought. It will become easier in time. She
just needed to find out what she wanted to do with her
life. She could make a phone call. She had a lifeline.

Chapter Four

Whistling a happy tune in her head, Jacqui surveyed her front yard. The grass, which had grown wild and untended the last couple of weeks, was trimmed and a gardener had spread soil along the path leading to the house. Jacqui had bought flowering plants, hoping the bloom would make the house feel homier.

A long time neighbor, Mrs. Higgins waved at her and then decided to come over for a chat. "Hello, Jacqui…" the old lady greeted her, holding tightly to the leash of her Boston terrier, Checkers. "Hi Mrs. Higgins," Jacqui answered happily, glad for the company. She knelt down and gave Checkers a scratch behind the ears.

"I see you're putting in some flowers," Mrs. Higgins smiled, "Nothing like a bunch of flowers to make one feel happy." "Yup," Jacqui agreed as she squirmed away from the dog, who was intent on licking her face. An awkward silence followed. Jacqui knew Mrs. Higgins wanted to give her some consoling words but was hesitant to talk about it.

"It was a horrible tragedy…I'm so sorry for you…" Mrs. Higgins managed to say. "I'm sorry too, Jacqui replied, "but things are getting better now." "Take all the time you need, Honey. It was a horrible thing that you went through. I don't know what's happening in the world. Right in your own home…" Mrs. Higgins muttered, shaking her head in disbelief.

Jacqui thanked the old lady and walked back to sit down by the porch steps. She was feeling better. Uncle Max's short visit a couple of days ago must have triggered something inside her brain. She had called her employer right after he left and asked if the offer for a vacation was still on. Her boss was more than glad to give it to her.

Jacqui had asked for two weeks leave. She then searched the yellow pages for a cleaning lady from out of town. She reckoned the woman wouldn't be as concerned that a murder had taken place right in her own home. But the service did request for higher rates coming from out of town.

Jacqui was more than glad to pay it. The cleaning lady had arrived the very next morning and stayed until everything was shiny and clean. They changed the curtains and removed the dusty covers from the throw pillows in the living room. The living room floors were waxed and vacuumed, and the linoleum kitchen floors polished until they shone.

For the first time in three months, Jacqui had entered her parents' bedroom. Everything was as it was on the night they were killed. Jacqui managed to put away her mom and dad's clothes in boxes to be picked up by a Goodwill truck. She was surprised by how very little personal stuff her father owned. There were no legal documents except the deed to the house, which Jacqui planned on securing in a safety deposit box.

Her mom was never much into fashion or make-up, never favored jewelry, and simply relied on an old wristwatch for an accessory. Jacqui fingered the watch and decided to keep it as a memento. When she entered Danny's room, Jacqui was suddenly assailed with a vicious loneliness. If her mom and dad had lived simply, Danny's room was filled with toys that could make a little boy very happy. His Play Station Portable 3000 rested on the bed, while a stack of DVD's of his favorite cartoons lay scattered on the floor.

Danny was prone to asthma attacks. Dad and mom made sure he was happy inside his room during those days he couldn't go out. That must have been why he was at home instead of in school during that fateful day. The thought brought sudden tears to Jacqui's eyes, which she brusquely brushed away. She didn't want the cleaning lady see her lose it. Happy over the clean house, Jacqui cooked some eggs smothered in cheese and brought it to the living room. She flicked on the TV and leaned back against the soft cushions. With the cleaning lady gone, she had the whole house to herself.

The soft drone of the television set was hypnotic. Exhaustion crept in. An exhausted Jacqui succumbed to the temptation and closed her eyes. She had probably fallen asleep when she felt a cold object press against her temple. Jacqui's eyes flew open. A dark figure stood beside her with a gun pointed into her face. Jacqui cringed in terror.

"We never leave unsettled business behind," the man said in a cold and cruel voice. Then he continued with a sneer, "It was a pleasure seeing your daddy scream when I shot your mom. His rage when I killed your little brother almost gave me an orgasm. Too bad, he won't see me do the same thing to you know now."

Jacqui screamed as a loud crash deafened her. She bolted upright and flailed her hands to defend herself. That's when she saw her uneaten plate of eggs littered on the floor. Broken pieces of plate glass scattered everywhere. The crash must have been what awakened her. She was all alone in the house.

Realizing she had a nightmare, Jacqui buried her face in her hands, crying softly. The house suffocated her. She couldn't breathe. The images of her family's slaughter played like a movie reel in her mind, torturing her. Foolishly she thought that she already had it under control.

A growing heat in her groin signaled what she desired most at this time. She needed to get laid again. It was the remedy her body craved for. Like an addict seeking an escape from reality, Jacqui entered her bedroom, took a quick shower, and rummaged through her closet.

Taking out a little black dress matched with pointy high-heeled shoes and a set of lace undies, Jacqui dressed hurriedly. She hoped to God there was a convention somewhere where she could find another random guy.

Brushing her hair vigorously until it shone and curled softly against her shoulder, Jacqui grabbed hold of a red lipstick. She moved closer to the mirror and stared at her eyes reflecting back at her. Is this really what you want to do, Jacqui? How long will you play this dangerous game before you get into trouble or catch some kind of disease? What if the next random guy turns out to be a creep and beats you up? Then what? Everything your dad worked for and died for is meaningless. Your dad was a hero. Every bad element he helped put away makes this world safer for others. And how do you honor your family's memory? By being a slut.

Jacqui stared at her own reflection for a long time. An idea was slowly forming in her head. An idea that could be the answer to the question she often asked herself these past few days. What do I really want to do with my life? Where do I go from here?

She had no boyfriend. No other family to make a connection with. She had lots of acquaintances at the office where she worked, but no close friends. She would be perfect for what she had in mind, because her absence wouldn't be noticed. She could train and be prepared to face the challenges. Yes, it seemed everything that had happened these last few months had led her toward the major decision that was slowly taking place inside her head.

And then a thought struck her. What if she came face to face with the murderer of her family? Would she recognize him? Everything that had happened that particular night was a blur in her memory. Instinctively, she knew she would recognize him when she saw him again. That kind of tragedy left its mark on the brain. Something about the way he had moved, perhaps? Jacqui wasn't sure how, but she vowed she would avenge her family someday.

As these thoughts crossed her mind, Jacqui noticed that she no longer felt the need to fuck someone. The urgent heat dissipated between her legs. In place of the sudden sexual pleasure her body craved, she felt determined. A steely resolve took control of her entire body.

She walked to the drawer and rummaged through the clothes within. Thrusting her arm deep within the recesses, her hand groped for a drawstring pouch that held a familiar object. Pulling the cloth bag out of its hiding place, Jacqui slid the string open and removed the cell phone within. She pressed the call button and heard the phone make a connection before it started ringing.

Jacqui waited with bated breath as the phone rang incessantly somewhere. She closed her eyes and hoped Uncle Max would pick up. Finally after what seemed like an eternity, she heard the click that signaled that the phone was now live in someone's hand.

"Hello…hello..." Jacqui spoke into the phone. There was only silence at the end of the open line. Jacqui instinctively knew her Uncle Max was there, listening. Without much ado, Jacqui stated her purpose.

"Uncle Max I know you can hear me. I've made a decision. You may not agree with me but if not with you, I'll go look for someone else who will take me in. Uncle Max, I've decided I want to be a bounty hunter too. Just like my daddy."

Jacqui didn't hear any reply. Only white noise filled the air before the phone was disconnected from the other end. But Jacqui wasn't worried. She knew Uncle Max had heard all she had to say. She took off her little black dress with a smirk on her face. She had no more use for it tonight. She kicked off her high-heels and removed all traces of make-up from her face before slipping on her pajamas.

She stepped out of her room and walked through the whole house, turning off the lights behind her as she passed through each room. She was no longer afraid.

There was a serene calmness in her face that hadn't been there before. This was the answer to her questions around why her family was killed. She believed everything happened for a purpose, and she had discovered her true purpose. Just like her dad before her, she would make this world a safer place for others. The thought made her smile.

Jacqui knew she could kick ass if she needed to.

-To be continued in Book 2-

If you enjoyed this title, I would appreciate your leaving a review of the book. Good reviews encourage an author to write as well as help books to sell. Good reviews can be just a few short sentences describing what you liked about the book without having a spoiler. If you could spend 30 seconds writing a review, I would appreciate it: you can review this title right now at your favorite retailer.

Here is a preview of the **next story** you may also enjoy:

Heart Surrendered: Obsessed Bounty Hunter Romance Series - Book 2

JACQUI CHUGGED the water from the container like a thirsty beast. She just couldn't get enough of it. Water never tasted so good, better than an orgasm, Jacqui thought, as she splashed some straight into her face. Jacqui was parched, grimy, and her body ached like she just came through a meat grinder. She was up at 0400 hours in her jogging suit and trainers. Uncle Max met her at the door of a building that resembled a huge hangar.

When Uncle Max said yesterday that training started today before the crack of dawn, Jacqui thought he meant some light exercises that would involve some sit-ups and jumping jacks. She was never further from the truth. The next couple of hours had been the most intensive Jacqui ever subjected her body to. And she knew this was just the start.

Uncle Max led her through a routine of squats and crunches, lunges and hamstring curls until her ass had no more feeling left in them. "C'mon Jacqui, move that body," Uncle Max shouted like a drill sergeant. Then he moved on to pull ups, sit-ups, bicep curls, and bench press. Her arms and legs felt disconnected from her body. Her hand was shaking so hard she almost dropped the water bottle she was holding. She was grateful for the fifteen minute break the old man gave her.

"Alright, Jacqui… back to work…" Uncle Max shouted from the sidelines.

She wanted to complain but didn't have the courage to. When she arrived yesterday, Uncle Max told her exactly what to expect for the next couple of weeks. He was dead serious as he went through the program with her. If he was trying to discourage her, he almost succeeded. But Jacqui was too proud to say it. She had come this far to become a bounty hunter.

Before she even got settled into the bedroom that would be hers during her stay, Uncle Max talked to her privately in what he called his 'interrogation room.' It was a small building at the back of the property. The walls were lined with an assortment of maps indicating the different states of the United States. There were yellow pins tacked on certain cities within the map. Jacqui looked around curiously. She noticed the different surveillance gadgets like GPS tracking, high resolution cameras, night vision goggles, an assortment of pens, and spy gear which she was seeing for the first time in her life.

A bank of television sets was stacked near the wall manned by a single individual. Jacqui saw it was streaming live from some part of the country she did not recognize. A huge glass cabinet held an assortment of guns, some she recognized from her dad's own collection.

"Take a seat Jacqui," Uncle Max indicated a wooden table with hardback chairs in a small corner of the room. He did not speak for some time and Jacqui had a strong desire to squirm under his intense gaze.

"Are you sure this is what you want because right now I am here to tell you, it's not going to be an easy life," Uncle Max said. Jacqui nodded her head, indicating she understood. When she came to her decision back home on the night she called Uncle Max, she quit her job the very next day. She told her boss she wanted to do some travelling. Her boss gave her the go-signal. "It's probably what you need right now," he even said.

Jacqui wasn't sure what Uncle Max thought about the whole idea. She hadn't heard from him since she made the call. But a few days later she found an envelope that was left on her porch. There was no forwarding address and it didn't look like it came by mail. Inside was a one-way ticket to Utah and strict instructions what to bring along. Only a small backpack was needed for the clothing list. It became pretty obvious this was not going to be some luxurious holiday.

She was met at the airport by a burly, bald-headed man, wearing dark sunglasses on a stern face. He reminded Jacqui of an ex-marine or military man. He ushered her into a waiting SUV, got behind the wheel, and started the engine.

They left the city behind until all Jacqui could see were tall mountain ranges in the distance. A few miles onward, they turned into a small dirt road and followed a winding path until Jacqui noticed a copse of large evergreen trees where they seemed to be headed. The trees covered a large expanse of land, save for small clearings with structures that resembled warehouses or large barns. They drove past these until they came to a smaller building where she saw Uncle Max waiting by the door. He greeted her warmly, but Jacqui sensed a certain formality in his demeanor.

Looking at him now, sitting behind the table with a grim expression on his face, Jacqui was suddenly filled with an overwhelming insecurity. Did she make the right decision after all? But Jacqui remembered the downward spiral she was on. The sex with random guys. The orgasms she needed to get some sleep so she could stop thinking about the tragic events of her life. And she needed a purpose… to find some meaning in her life. To honor her dad's memory so she would never forget. For her mom who supported him all the way, and for Danny, who was never given the chance to experience what life was all about.

"Yes, Uncle Max. I have never been surer about anything in my life," she declared with a certain degree of conviction. Uncle Max smiled, and for the first time since she arrived, Jacqui felt relieved. She knew whatever lay ahead, Uncle Max wouldn't spare her, wouldn't try to make things easy for her. She knew that.

"Ok then, let's get you started. I am The Agency. I will be responsible for your training. You will not question my decisions… you will do as I say. The training will be rigorous because you will meet all kinds of low-life scumbags. A lot of times your life will be in danger. But you will be trained in self-defense and handling weapons until I feel that you are totally capable of protecting yourself out there. Then and only then will I send you out on a mission. Is that clear?"

Uncle Max asked. Jacqui nodded her head in agreement.

"Alright, settle in. You will be shown to your room. Tomorrow your training starts. And for the next couple of days you will only remember pain," The old man warned her. He wasn't kidding. After five hours of the most intense exercise routines she had ever done, Jacqui couldn't even remember her name. Her body hurt even in places she didn't know existed. And this was just her first day in boot camp.

Lunch had been sparse, with just some fish and vegetables. She was given an hour to rest inside her room which was composed of a bunk bed and a footlocker for her personal stuff. No TV, no telephone, no computer or laptop. Then she was called back again and told to run around a circuit she didn't even notice earlier in the day. She tried counting in her head the number of times she completed a circuit before fatigue settled in and lost count completely. It took all her will power to put one leg in front of the other. By the time Uncle Max called for a halt, dusk had settled and stars appeared brightly in a cloudless sky.

"Supper will be brought to your room. Tomorrow we do the whole routine again," Uncle Max declared before he left. It wasn't a request. It was an order. Jacqui trudged slowly back to her room. There is no time to dwell on the unfamiliarity and sparse surroundings. The bed was a most welcome sight and calling her name. She groaned in pain as she stretched her arms over her head to remove her workout clothes.

Her back was racked with pain as she bent to unlace her trainers.

Jacqui managed to splash some water onto her face before falling face down into the soft covers with only her undies on. Sleep came easy for Jacqui that night. A sleep so deep she hardly noticed the appearance of two figures in her room.

"You think she'll make it?" an older voice inquired. "I don't know Uncle Max. You put her through the wringer today," the other replied. Uncle Max sighed as he looked at the sleeping form of the girl on the bed. "You're hoping maybe she'll give up and just go back home?" the second figure asked curiously.

"Yes… this kind of life isn't for her. She's been through a lot already. But I also can't accept throwing her life away with all those men in strange hotel rooms," Uncle Max replied. "Well… you said the same thing about me too, remember? I didn't turn out too badly," the younger man said. "No, Adam, you are doing very well. The fact is… you will play an important role in this girl's future," Uncle Max replied.

"I can hardly wait…" Adam replied, taking in the full breasts and rounded ass of the sleeping form on the bed. "Just learn to keep that cock of yours inside your pants…" warned the old man, with a hint of indulgence in his voice.

The two figures departed slowly out of the room where Jacqui Schneider slept an exhausted, dreamless sleep.

If you enjoyed this preview then look for **Heart Surrendered: Obsessed Bounty Hunter Romance Series - Book 2**.

Here is a preview of **another story** you may enjoy:

Fifty Recipes For Disaster: A New Adult Romance Series - Book 1

"**ALL RIGHT**, chefs, you have ninety seconds to get your food plated and presented. If your dish isn't ready, you will automatically be eliminated."

My cooking instructor, Chef Michelle Lee, walks through the room, examining our stations. My fellow cooking students and I are competing for the chance to enter another competition. The winner of today's cooking challenge will get the chance to compete for a full-time apprenticeship at Fission, one of Austin's hottest restaurants.

I'm not confident in many aspects of my life, but I know I dominate in the kitchen. I begin plating my dish just as Chef Lee approaches my station.

"Your food presents beautifully as usual, Kiara," she tells me with a smile. "If it tastes as good as it looks, you've got this in the bag," she adds with a soft whisper.

The instructors at *Le Cordon Bleu College of Culinary Arts* aren't supposed to show favoritism to their students, but Chef Lee keeps a soft spot for me. Along with being one of my teachers, she's also my faculty adviser, and she knows the unusual circumstances that brought me to the school.

"Time's up," she calls out to the class. "Place your finished plates on the head table."

I walk my plate to the front of the room and place it on top of the placard that holds my student ID number. My classmates follow suit… several of them glare at me after looking at my dish. I am delighted, knowing they're all both jealous and impressed I was able to execute a well-developed *Cioppino* within the given time frame. My rich seafood stew is accompanied by fresh sourdough loaves. I examine my classmates' dishes and feel my chances of winning are good.

"Clear away your stations," Chef Lee directs. "Chef Lawton will be here shortly to judge your plates, and I don't want any evidence of who made what on display when he arrives."

Chef Lawton is the *sous* chef at Fission and the judge of this stage of the apprenticeship competition. I clear my station quickly and then I take a seat at the front of the room. I want to be able to see Chef Lawton's expressions as he tastes each dish.

As I sit nervously in my chair, my classmates finish clearing their stations. I can tell everyone else is just as anxious as I am… we've received plenty of critiques from our instructors but this will be the first time a professional chef from a restaurant will be tasting our food. The door of the classroom opens and a tall man wearing a black chef's jacket enters the room.

"Chef Lawton, it's so lovely to see you," Chef Lee welcomes him. "I can't tell you how excited we are to participate in this competition."

"We're excited as well," Chef Lawton replies. "We're always looking for new, innovative chefs at

Fission. I'm looking forward to tasting the dishes and welcoming one of your students into the final leg of the competition. I see that all of the plates are ready. If it's all right with you, I'll get started."

"Of course," Chef Lee agrees.

I try not to hold my breath as I watch Chef Lawton sample each of the plates. I feel encouraged when he reaches mine. Instead of sampling one bite and moving on, he holds the broth in his mouth for a moment, and then tastes each type of seafood in turn. The expression on his face tells me that my stew is perfect, and I say a silent prayer I haven't been out-cooked by any of my classmates.

"First off, I'd like to say this is an impressive display," the seasoned chef begins. "Everything on this table is up to par with the level of skill and talent I expect to see from second-year students. That being said, there is a clear winner. One chef not only executed a delicious dish, but also added a few subtle, original touches that showed innovation and creativity."

Adrenaline rushes through me as he moves to stand behind my dish. "Who created this *Cioppino*?" he asks.

I blush involuntarily as I raise my hand.

"And what is your name, Chef?"

"Kiara Sands," I reply, trying to mask the excitement in my voice.

"Well, Chef Sands, it's an honor to welcome you to the next stage of the competition. I look forward to tasting more of your food as the weeks progress. I am needed back at Fission, but Chef Lee will provide you with the details of your new position." He turns to the rest of the class. "To the rest of you, don't be discouraged. You all provided me with excellent dishes, and you have bright futures ahead of you."

"Thank you, Chef," the class responds in unison.

Chef Lawton makes a quick exit, and Chef Lee takes his place behind the head table. "Excellent work today, class. You're dismissed until tomorrow," she announces. My classmates gather their things and leave the room… I stay behind to talk to Chef Lee.

"Kiara, I'm so proud of you." She beams once we are alone. "As you know, there will be two other chefs competing with you at Fission. You're the only one who's been selected from *Le Cordon Bleu*, and I know you'll represent us well." She moves to her desk and pulls a large package from her bottom drawer. "Here is your apprenticeship packet. You'll receive your Fission jacket when you report for work tomorrow morning. If you have any questions, or just need someone to talk to, you know where to reach me."

"This seems like a wonderful dream, and part of me is afraid that I'll wake up any minute now," I confess.

Chef Lee gives me a maternal smile. "This is a dream, Kiara. It's your dream. And you're well on *your* way to achieving it."

<<◇>>

The information packet Chef Lee presented me with instructs me to be at Fission at 10:00 am. I check my dashboard clock as I pull into the parking lot... 9:40 am. I feel smug, knowing I'm probably the first of the three competitors to arrive. I check my makeup in the rear-view mirror before exiting my car.

Fission is housed in a modern brick building in East Austin, one of the city's burgeoning hipster areas. The area gives off a relaxed, laid-back vibe, but I know the kitchen of Fission will be anything but.

I push open the heavy, solid oak door and am greeted by a pixy-sized hostess with spiked, lavender hair.

"Table for one?" she asks me brightly.

"No," I reply nervously. "My name is Kiara Sands. I'm supposed to start work today."

"Oh! You're one of the newbies!" She says warmly. "I'm Megan. It's a pleasure to meet you. The other two are already here. I'll show you to their table."

Damn it! I'd been so sure I'd make the best impression by arriving first, and here I am, the last of the apprentices to report for our first day.

Megan seems to sense my disappointment. "Don't worry. Paul doesn't give a shit how early people show up. As long as you're here when you're scheduled, you'll be fine. And you haven't missed anything. The other two have just been sitting alone since they got here," she offers reassuringly.

"Thank you for that," I say half-heartedly. As I follow Megan through the restaurant, I'm struck by the eclectic, well-placed décor. All of the tables are made of the same polished oak as the front door. The water goblets on the tabletops are tinted in hues of blue, green, and rose… a selection of art from all around the world adorns the walls. The ambiance is on the right side of the fine line between cozy and overwhelming. The restaurant offers a large main dining room, with smaller, more private rooms on each side.

"This is a beautiful place," I say as Megan leads me toward the back of the main room.

"It is," she agrees. "Paul handled all of the decorating himself. He says that Austin is a melting pot, and he wants all of our customers to feel at home when they dine here."

I'm about to comment on how successfully that goal had been achieved when we arrive at a table occupied by a beautiful blonde woman and a swarthy man with sandy blond hair. A pot of coffee and three cups sit on the table.

"Kiara Sands, this is Jenny Foster and Robbs Martin," Megan introduces us. She checks her watch before speaking again. "It's a quarter to ten, so I imagine that Paul will be out shortly. I suggest you get fully caffeinated and enjoy this time off your feet. It will be the last one for today," she warns with a friendly, knowing tone.

I take a seat in the chair next to Jenny as Megan moves back to the hostess station. "It's a pleasure to meet you both," I offer.

"It's a pleasure to meet you too," Robbs replies. "Congratulations on making it this far in the competition. And I'd like to apologize right now for how thoroughly I'm going to kick both of your asses. This job is mine." He speaks with a blend of arrogance and sarcasm, and I can tell immediately that Robbs and I are not going to get along.

Personal relationships are something I struggle with. In my experience, there's no point in getting close to someone who will inevitably let you down. I prefer to keep my head down and focus on getting my job done. As Chef Lee said yesterday, I have a dream and I'm well on my way to achieving it. I'll be damned if I let Robbs or anyone else get in my way.

"Just ignore Robbs," Jenny advises me. "He thinks that he's God's gift to food... women too, probably." She giggles. "So Kiara, what's your story? Which campus were you plucked from?"

"I'm in my second year at *Le Cordon Bleu*," I answer with pride. In my opinion, *Le Cordon Bleu* is the best culinary school in the area—it's also the hardest to get in to. Jenny seems impressed by my background, but Robbs laughs and dismisses it immediately.

"The *Bleu* is all right, I guess," he snorts, "if you're happy being complacent and doing everything old-school."

"I wasn't aware that being classically trained is a bad thing," I reply shortly. "Tell me, what culinary Mecca do you hail from?"

"*Escoffier*," he answers with a cocky smile. "You know, where all of the innovative, cutting-edge people attend. Three of my instructors were nominated for the James Beard award. So like I said, no hard feelings, but I'm going to kick both of your asses. *Escoffier* specializes in farm-to-table cuisine, so I'm exactly the kind of chef Fission is looking for."

I dismiss his statement with a glare. While the *Auguste Escoffier School of Culinary Arts* is reputed for turning out fantastic chefs, in some culinary circles it's dismissed as a hipster college that prioritizes food trends over basic technique and skill.

I don't feel like debating the merits of my education with Robbs, so I turn to Jenny. "And where do you go?" I ask pleasantly.

"The Art Institute," she replies. "I'm still not positive that cooking is my life's passion. I wanted to go to a college that offers other programs, in case I decided to change my major."

"If you're not sure that you want to be a chef, then what the fuck are you doing here?" Robbs asks hotly. "You should give your spot to someone who knows that this is what they want."

Jenny's green eyes fill with both anger and embarrassment, and I can tell she's fumbling for a response.

"I don't agree with that at all," I say warmly. "What better way to find out if you enjoy working in a real kitchen, than by actually doing it?"

"That's exactly what my instructor said when I won this spot," Jenny says with a nod.

"I see how it's going to be," Robbs interjects with more sarcasm. "The two of you are going to band together in 'sisterhood' and gang up on me."

"That's not how it's going to be at all," a firm voice says from behind me. I turn to see one of the most attractive men I've ever laid my eyes on. He's tall, with broad shoulders, blue eyes, and sandy blond hair. He's also wearing a black chef's jacket, identical to the one Chef Lawton wore when he judged my dish. He holds eye contact with me for several moments before he speaks again.

"This competition will come down to one thing and one thing only... the quality of your food. Only one of you will be named my new apprentice, so ganging up on each other won't serve any purpose. I'm Paul Weston, and I'd like to welcome you to my restaurant." He extends his hand to me.

I respond with a firm handshake and a smile. "I'm Kiara Sands. Thank you for this opportunity."

"You're here because you deserve to be. No thanks are necessary," he assures me.

If you enjoyed this sample then look for **Fifty Recipes For Disaster: A New Adult Romance Series - Book 1**.

Here is a preview of **another story** you may enjoy:

Romeo Alpha: A BBW Paranormal Shifter Romance - Book 1 by Darla Dunbar

AMANDA WONDERED how the hell she had gotten so far away from home. When she walked, she usually didn't go past a couple of blocks, but she felt so different today. Something was pushing her further and in a different direction, and she wasn't sure what it was. But she didn't care at the moment, because she just wanted to walk.

Not thinking twice about where she was going, she let her gut instinct give her the direction she needed.

Her grandmother had always told her to go with her gut. She'd said human instinct was better than anything. "Intuition is a girl's best friend," she would say, and then they would both laugh. Talks she and her grandmother had always seemed to pop into her head at the strangest of times, like now.

Here she was, going for a walk, and wondering why she wanted to go in a different direction, and there was her grandmother's voice in her head, propelling her along. Amanda missed her grandmother more with every passing year.

Amanda paused and thought about her life thus far. She had just graduated from college and started working in the local animal hospital, but it wasn't quite like she had thought. She didn't see the care and passion she'd hoped to find in the industry. In the city, being a vet was all about how much money you could make, how many pets you could treat. And, at twenty-four, it was hard to be taken seriously.

Her two female roommates were nice, but they all just went their separate ways. They didn't eat ice cream and watch movies like on *Friends*. They didn't share secrets or even laugh or hang out. They really just slept in the same apartment, and they usually weren't even home at the same time. Except Amanda, that is.

Amanda was always at home, it seemed. She had nowhere else to go, really. The other two girls spent most nights out with their real friends or their boyfriends. Amanda lived a lonely life, but she was happy. At least, she was pretty sure she was happy. After all, she had an upstanding career, and she still had money left over from her savings.

Both her parents had been killed in a car accident years ago. Amanda had graduated from high school with no family there that day or on the day she graduated from college. It was what it was, though, and she knew that her parents watched her from Heaven.

The only positive thing was that her parents had been prepared and had made sure they left enough money and a big enough life insurance policy to help her out. They would be surprised but happy knowing how much that money had helped her in the years after their death. She was proud to say that she was able to live off of it through her college years. She'd never even had to get a job like most kids did. Amanda had been able to focus on her classes.

That freedom wasn't worth it, though. She would have worked three jobs at a time while going to school for one more day with her parents.

However, the account was finally starting to dry up, and she needed to think about what she would do. Sure, she had a new job that could pay her bills, but those loans were piling up with interest. Even a vet job only went so far.

Amanda sighed as she began the trek back toward the house.

Amanda liked her walks in the evening. It helped her to relax, enjoying the quiet time alone. And while Amanda wasn't overweight by any means, it helped slim her waistline, which showed those extra biscuits she liked every now and again.

She turned and began to make her way back to the townhouse she shared with her roommates, but stopped as she heard a noise.

A rustling came from behind her, and she turned to see the bushes shaking. Looking over to the other side of the sidewalk, she saw those bushes shake as well. Not wanting to wait around to find out what was behind the leaves, she took off at a run. She swore she heard a growl come from behind her, but she didn't turn to see what was chasing her. That would only slow her down. As she reached the door to her home, she quickly turned the knob and went through headfirst. Shutting the door quickly, she looked out the window. She got a glimpse of a long black furry tail as something ran around to the side of her building.

"What in the world are you doing, Amanda?" Betsy stood there looking at her inquisitively.

"Something was chasing me."

"What?"

"I don't know what it was, but something big and furry was chasing me. I saw a long black tail just now when I walked into the house."

"You mean when you dove into the house?" Betsy's grin faded. "I'll call the game warden. If there is a big animal outside, then none of us need to go out there until they find it and get rid of it."

"Well, I don't want them to kill it."

"I know, silly, but if it's a wild animal, they can take it out to the National Forest and let it loose. The city is no place for a wild animal." Betsy turned and picked up the phone from the receiver.

Amanda stood in shocked silence as she listened to her roommate tell the person on the other end of the phone what had happened.

She knew from Betsy's tone that she and the person on the other end of the phone were questioning her sanity. They lived in a big city, and the closest thing they got to a wild animal was a stray cat or two. They didn't even get raccoons. If there was some huge animal like she thought, then it would make headline news.

Shaking her head in aggravation, Amanda turned toward her room. She suddenly felt silly and didn't want to have to explain what she saw to any more people.

"Amanda? Where are you going? They are on their way and might need to talk to you."

"Tell them it was a dog. Now that I'm thinking about it, it kind of looked like that couple that lives down the road's greyhound. Maybe he just got out."

"Are you sure, Amanda?" Betsy asked, turning and saying something into the phone.

Without saying another word, Amanda shut the door to her room tight and then quickly locked the door. She looked over her room and, seeing the window open and the curtains blowing in the breeze, she ran over to push the window pane down and lock it tight. As she stood there, she looked out into the woods that made up her backyard. There, in the distance, two yellow eyes stared back at her.

Suddenly, more eyes appeared, and it seemed the animals went on forever. She was amazed, since the woods behind her house were very dense and small. The dark night was lit with a full moon. A shiver raced through her as she stood there and stared into the first set of yellow eyes. She quickly shut the curtains and went to sit on her bed. She didn't think she would ever be able to fall asleep knowing what was out there. As she laid her head on the pillow, her mind wondered to large beasts with yellow eyes and sharp fangs. But she was soon fast asleep.

<<<>>>

Amanda awoke with a yawn. It had been almost a month since the incident with what she now called a dog. She had agreed with Betsy that her mind had been playing tricks on her that night. There were often times when she was sure she felt eyes on her, and she would turn in one direction or another, looking. What she was seeking, she didn't know, but somewhere in the back of her mind, she just wanted to know if the eyes she had seen that night had been real or just part of her dreams that evening. She was still so uneasy about it that her walks seemed to get earlier and earlier each evening.

She was just about to walk out the door when her phone started ringing. She quickly grabbed it and pushed the button to answer it.

"Hello."

"Ms. Walker?"

"Yes?"

"Hello, Ms. Walker, my name is Ernest Montgomery. I am calling to tell you that your aunt has passed away."

"My aunt? But I don't have any family. You must have the wrong Ms. Walker."

"No, ma'am. Your father was Joshua Walker, correct? Mother Maureen Walker?"

"Yes."

"Then, I have the right Ms. Walker. It is your father's sister I am referring to. She unexpectedly passed away from a heart attack. I am very sorry for your loss."

"Oh, my gosh! I never knew I even had any family. I am very sad that I didn't get to meet her."

"Yes, ma'am. I'm sure. She was a nice woman. I have also called you to see if you can meet with me. I need to go over her will with you."

"Her will?"

"Yes, ma'am. Your aunt was a wealthy woman."

"Oh? Um, okay. When would you like to meet?"

"The sooner, the better."

"Okay. How about today?"

"That would be great. I am in Slatesville, in the valley."

"Oh. Okay. That is just forty-five minutes from me. I can be there in a couple of hours."

"Sounds good, ma'am. I am at the *Montgomery Law Firm*. I am the only attorney in the town."

"Okay. Thank you, sir. I will see you soon."

"Yes, ma'am. I'll be waiting."

Amanda fell back on the couch, stunned, for what seemed like forever. Everything was pushed to the back of her mind as she thought about what she had just learned. She had a family. Well, she *did* have a family. Now her aunt was gone. Could there be others in her family who she knew nothing about? She didn't know, but she did know one thing. She wasn't going to find out sitting around here, twiddling her thumbs. She needed to get going fast.

Amanda headed for the kitchen. She wasn't surprised to see that no one was there. Of course her roommates weren't home. They were either in class or with their boyfriends.

Smiling, she made a cup of coffee and drank it slowly, thinking about what she might find out. Then, with a deep sigh, she made her way to her car. She looked at the small Honda with pride. It was a pile of junk to some, but it held a special place in her heart. She hadn't been able to get rid of her father's car. Instead, she had sold her own.

She looked down at the small picture he had taped to the dash near the speedometer. She was about six in the picture, and she had been holding her mom's cheeks in her hands as she kissed her.

She remembered the day like it was yesterday. They had just got to a cabin they vacationed in. She had enjoyed herself so much. The little cabin had one bedroom with a queen-sized bed where her parents slept and a set of bunk beds for her. They had stayed up late roasting marshmallows as her father told her scary stories about wolves and vampires. She had ended up in their bed, snuggled between the two of them. They had spent the next day hiking and walking trails and seeing tons of waterfalls and animals.

She had loved it and had never forgotten. It soon became a family tradition to go camping every year. After some of those trips, they didn't return home.

Instead, they moved on to a different location. The constant moving had been hard on her as a kid, but she would have never told her parents that. She had felt like they were hiding something from her. Of course, she had been young back then and had blown it off as childhood curiosity. Now, with this new family member, she wasn't so sure.

Her parents had been very quiet people. They seemed cautious of everything going on around them and were even a little jumpy at times. Maybe there was more going on here than she thought. She needed to find out.

She wiped away a tear and go in the car. The car had a huge dent in one side and was almost fifteen years old, but it got her where she needed to go. She slid the car into drive and smiled to herself.

"Dad would be proud that his car was still running so good, wouldn't he, Trixy?" She and her father had named the car together.

Amanda turned onto the next road and made her way down the narrow two-lane road that led into the mountains. She had never been this way because her parents always went the long way around the mountains. They said they liked to take the scenic route.

She came to a small wooden sign that said *Slatesville—Welcome to your home away from home*. She smiled at the welcoming sign and kept on her way to the town. As she drove, she was amazed at how beautiful everything was. The low-hanging branches of the trees scraped the roof of the car every once in a while.

She was amazed at how many animals she saw. Deer acted as if they weren't afraid of her car. Raccoons were plentiful, and she jumped when a large black snake slithered across the road. There were people all around, and they watched her car curiously as she made her way down the street.

The town reminded her of a long lost western ghost town. It was a little spooky, and she caught herself checking the doors to make sure they were locked. The men nodded at her as she moved forward and many of the people smiled, although they held themselves back a little.

Amanda finally saw the sign that said *Montgomery Law Firm*. She pulled into one of the many vacant parking spots and slowly got out of the car. A handsome man leaned against the building she was about to enter. His brown eyes had flecks of yellow and orange in their deep depths. She smiled slightly, and the man just continued to stare as he looked her over slowly.

"Can I help you, ma'am?"

"I am just here to see Mr. Montgomery."

"Well, you're in the right place, Miss…?"

"Oh, Amanda. Amanda Walker. And you are?"

Something changed in his eyes as he smiled at her and made his way to her side. He held out his hand to her. "Name's Curtis Livingston."

"Oh. Do you live here?"

"Yes. I'm one of the controlling partners here in Slatesville. Well, I have to be going. It was good to meet you."

"You, too, Mr. Livingston."

"Please, call me Curt. Everyone does."

"Only if you call me Amanda."

"That's a deal, sweet lady." She flushed all over when he raised her hand to his lips and gently caressed her knuckles with a brief touch of his mouth. She felt the rise in temperature in her cheeks spread across her upper chest. She stood there and watched as he walked away from her down the street to slip inside a store. She felt foolish and realized that she had been staring. She shook her head, trying to think straight and clear the thoughts that were running through her mind.

Amanda was always aware that she wasn't the Barbie doll type of girl. Although she wasn't fat, she wasn't rail thin, which most men liked, either. Her waist and stomach didn't look like a washboard, although it didn't look like a bunch of bread dough either.

She instantly felt inadequate and quickly turned around to walk to the door of the attorney's office. Knocking, she was surprised when the door instantly opened. The man who opened the door wasn't what she expected. Mr. Montgomery was a short, pudgy man. He didn't wear a business suit, and he didn't seem stuffy at all. He was older and had a short goatee around his mouth. His hair was pulled back into a ponytail at the back of his neck, and he smiled when he saw her.

"You must be Amanda. You look just like your father, except for your eyes. You have your mother's eyes. Let's hope you didn't inherit your father's temper, though," he chuckled.

"You knew my father?"

"Oh, why yes, my dear. We grew up together, Josh and I. Have to say we got into a lot of trouble as kids, and your aunt Mabel was always there to wag her finger and tell on us. You see, there were the three of us; Joshua, Jeremiah, and I. We were called the three musketeers. Mabel wanted to be the fourth, but you know boys. We would never let her, so she always ran and told on us to get back at us for not including her; the little minx." He told the story fondly, and she instantly knew that this man held her family in the highest regard. She also knew he was her ticket to finding out the truth about her family.

"Do I have any more family that I don't know of?" She held her breath, as though she were a child again, asking if Santa Claus was real.

"I am sure you do, my dear. Unfortunately, your aunt was the last of your father's line. She couldn't have any children, and most of the family was killed in a fire in '90. I am sure there is still family on your mother's side, though. However, I must warn you that they are not the kind of people you want to know. Now, if you will come in, I will tell you about everything that now belongs to you."

"What?"

"Oh, my dear, you must know that your father's family had a legacy. You are the only Traverse left to take over the family business."

"What? I don't know what you're talking about."

"They never did tell you who you really are, did they? Oh, you poor child. I am afraid you are going to learn some things about yourself that are going to be hard for you. You must still be a virgin as well."

"I beg your pardon, sir, but I don't see how that's any of your damn business."

"No, my dear, I do not mean to be crude. I was just saying that you have never undergone the Change. It will happen, though. You recently turned twenty-four, and everything changes now."

"What change? What in the hell are you talking about?"

"They hid that from you, too? Oh my gosh. You don't know? Oh, Lord. Okay, first things first. You are now the owner of your family's estate."

"Family estate? So I have a house."

He smiled kindly at her. "Not just a house, my dear. It is what holds the legacy of your family name together. The estate has fifteen bedrooms with their own bathrooms and fireplaces, a kitchen, dining room, parlor, living area, office, library, Carolina room, staff quarters, wrap-around porch with two different sections screened in, pool, tennis courts and 300 acres. It was the pride and joy of your ancestor, Edgar. He was a distant grandfather of yours."

"Oh my gosh."

"Yes, ma'am. How about this? How about I get the keys and directions to the place? You go take a look at it, and then we can talk tomorrow about what you want to do. Stephan has been looking over things, and since your aunt's death, he has given everyone time off until you arrive and decide where to go from there."

Amanda wasn't sure she had the energy to deal with all of this tonight. "Unfortunately, it is very late. Is there somewhere that I can stay for a couple days and then I can go from there and take the day tomorrow to go look at the place?"

"That is perfect. Just give me a second, and I'll find a place for you to stay tonight."

Amanda sat quietly and listened to him talk on his phone. She didn't even hear his words as she thought of what she was going to do.

"I have gotten you a little cabin to rent down the road," he said, drawing her attention back to him. "It is in the woods a little but has electricity and such. On such short notice, I couldn't find anything else. It is only about ten minutes away. The key will be under the mat at the front door. Just go on in and make yourself at home."

"That is perfect. Thank you so much."

"You're welcome, my dear, and we will talk tomorrow. Say ten o'clock tomorrow morning? We will meet here and go to see the house together."

"Perfect. Thank you, Mr. Montgomery."

If you enjoyed this sample then look for **Romeo Alpha: A BBW Paranormal Shifter Romance - Book 1 by Darla Dunbar**.

Other Books by Carla Coxwell

- Torrid Exposure New Adult Romance Series

- Devil's Advocate BBW MC New Adult Romance Series

- Fifty Recipes For Disaster New Adult Romance Series

- Star Bright New Adult Romance Series

Get the latest update on new releases from the author at:

https://www.carlacoxwell.com/newsletter

About the Author - Carla Coxwell

Carla has always been a fan of romance novels. To augment what she made waiting on tables to help her way through college, Carla also did some freelance work in the romance genre.

Now she enjoys living vicariously through her characters in her New Adult Romance books.

Connect with Carla Coxwell

I really appreciate you reading my book! Here are my social media coordinates:

Friend me on Facebook:
https://www.facebook.com/CarlaCoxwell/

Follow me on Twitter: https://twitter.com/carlacoxwell

Check me out on Goodreads:
https://www.goodreads.com/author/show/10691544.Carla_Coxwell

Subscribe to my newsletter:
https://www.carlacoxwell.com/newsletter/

Visit my website: https://www.carlacoxwell.com/

9 781987 863680